THIS WALKER BOOK BELONGS TO:

Jessica

First published 1997 by Walker Books Ltd
87 Vauxhall Walk, London SE11 5HJ

This edition published 1998

4 6 8 10 9 7 5 3

This book has been typeset in Calligraphic 810.

Printed in Hong Kong

British Library Cataloguing in Publication Data
A catalogue record for this book is available from the British Library.

ISBN 0-7445-6035-7

GINGER

Charlotte Voake

WALKER BOOKS
AND SUBSIDIARIES
LONDON • BOSTON • SYDNEY

Ginger was a lucky cat.

He lived with
a little girl
who made him
delicious
meals

and gave him
a beautiful basket,

where he would curl up ...

and close
his eyes.

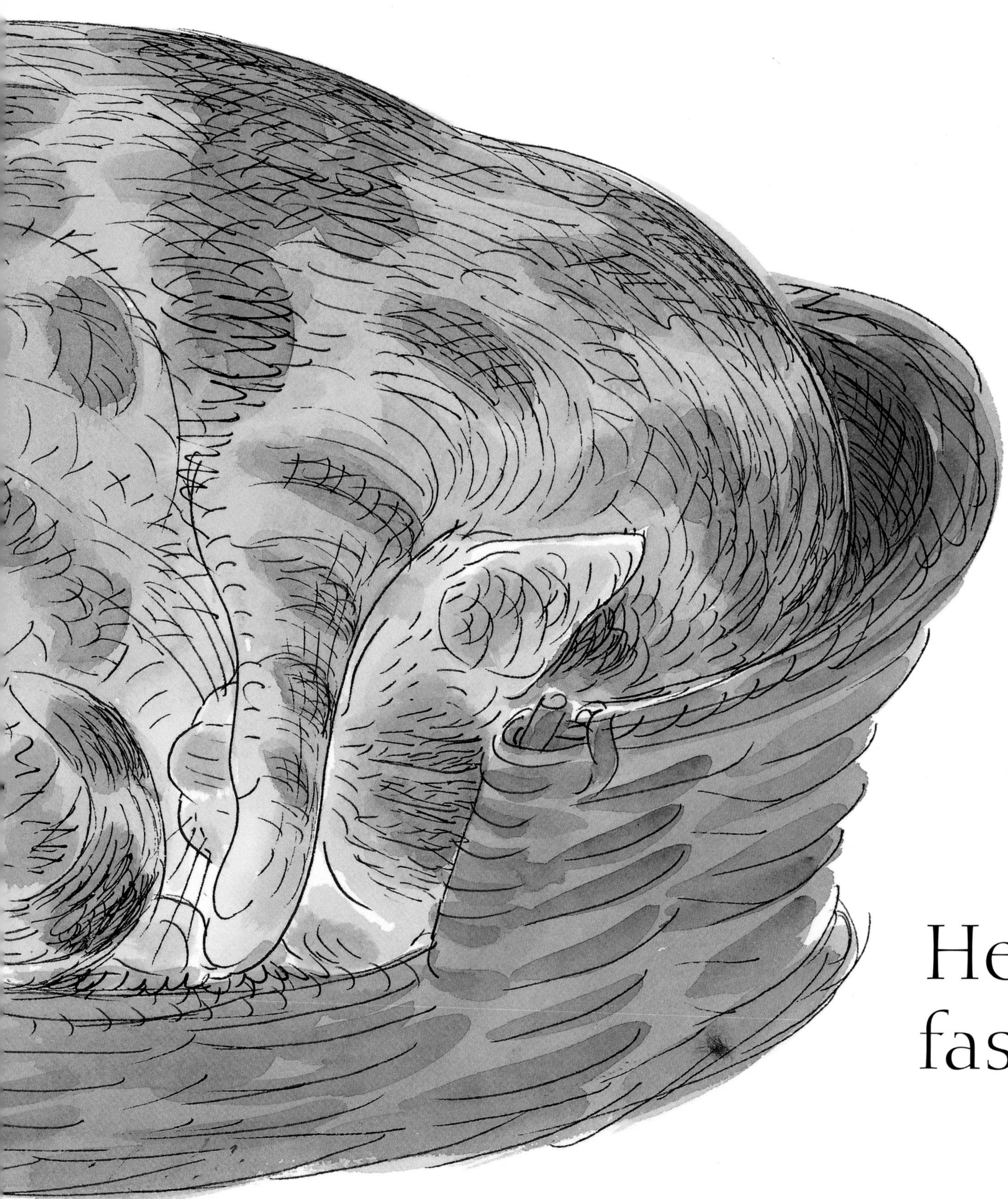

Here he is,
fast asleep.

But here he is again,
WIDE AWAKE.

What's this?

A kitten!

“He'll be a nice new friend for you, Ginger,” said the little girl.

But Ginger
didn't want a new friend,
especially one like this.
Ginger hoped the
kitten would
go away,

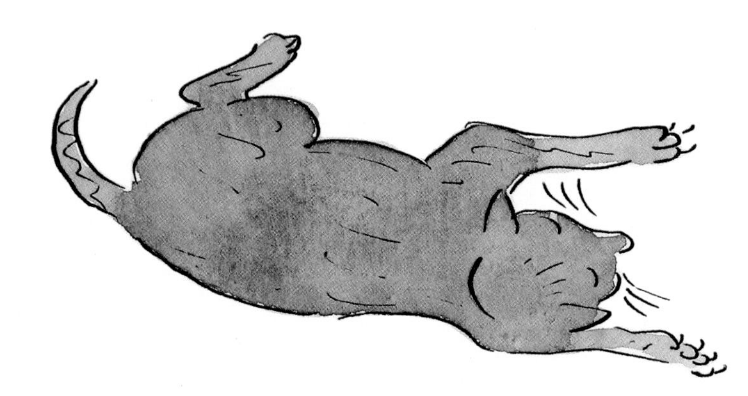

but he didn't.

Everywhere
Ginger went,
the kitten followed,
springing out
from behind
doors,

leaping on to Ginger's back,

even eating
Ginger's food!

What a naughty
kitten!

But what upset Ginger
more than anything
was that whenever
he got into his
beautiful basket,
the kitten always
climbed in too,

and
the little
girl didn't
do anything
about it.

So Ginger decided to leave home.

He went out
through the cat flap
and he didn't come back.

The kitten waited for a bit,
then he got into
Ginger's basket.

It wasn't the same without Ginger.

The little girl
found him on the table
drinking some milk.

"You naughty kitten!" she said.

"I thought you
were with Ginger.
Where is he anyway?"

She looked
in Ginger's
basket,

but of course he wasn't there.

“Perhaps
he’s eating
his food,”
she said.

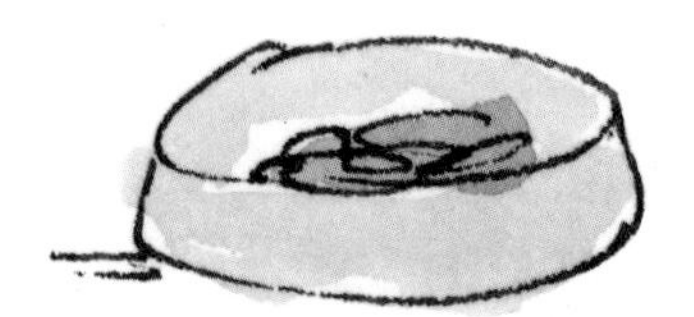

But Ginger
wasn’t there
either.

"I hope
he's not
upset,"
she said.

"I hope
he hasn't
run away."

She put on her
wellingtons
and went out
into the
garden,
and that
is where
she found
him;

a very wet,
sad, cold Ginger,
hiding under
a bush.

The little girl carried Ginger and the kitten inside. "It's a pity you can't be friends," she said.

She gave Ginger a special meal.

She gave the kitten
a little plate
of his own.

So when the little girl
went in to see
the two cats
again,

THIS is how she found them.

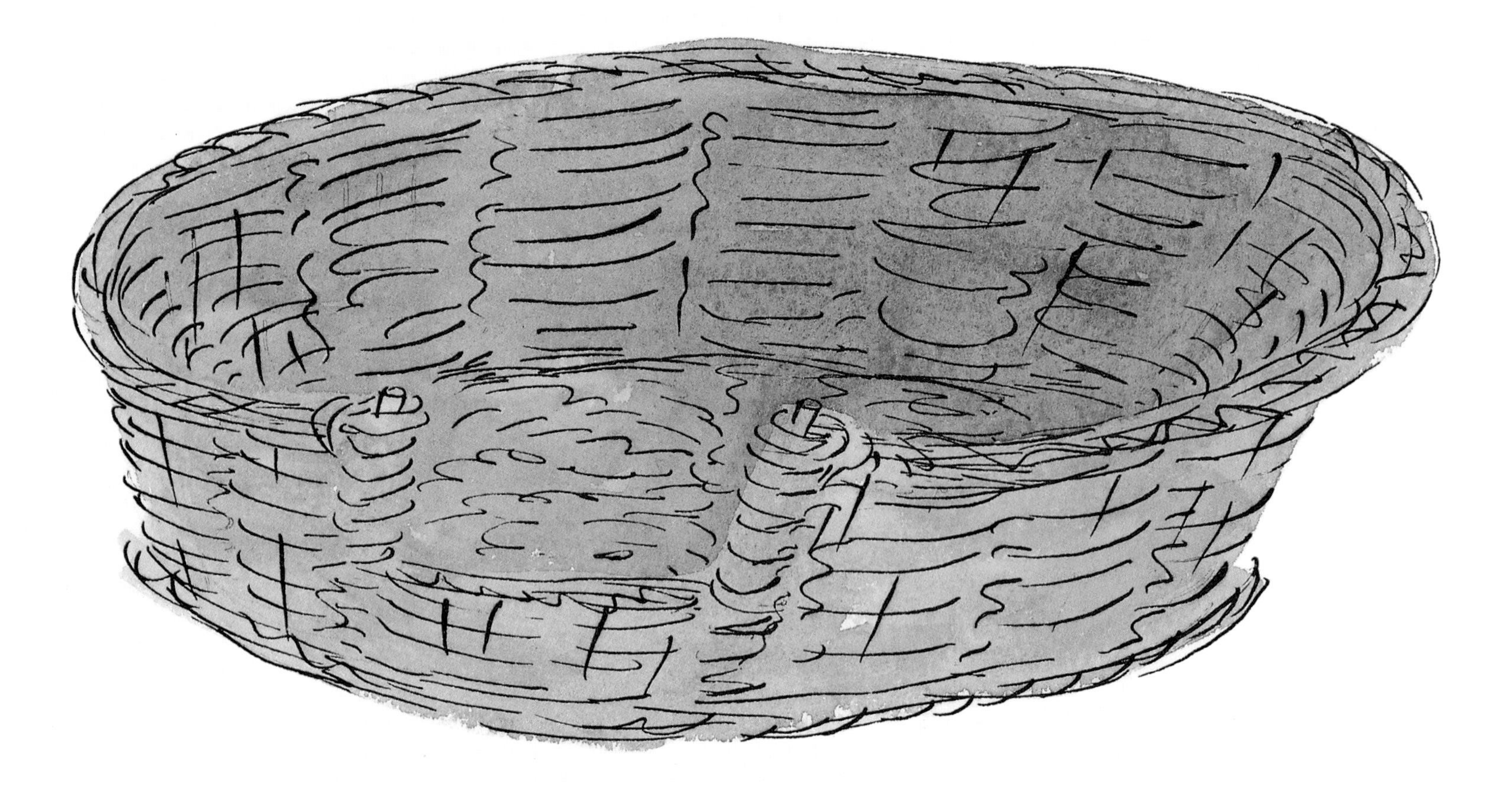

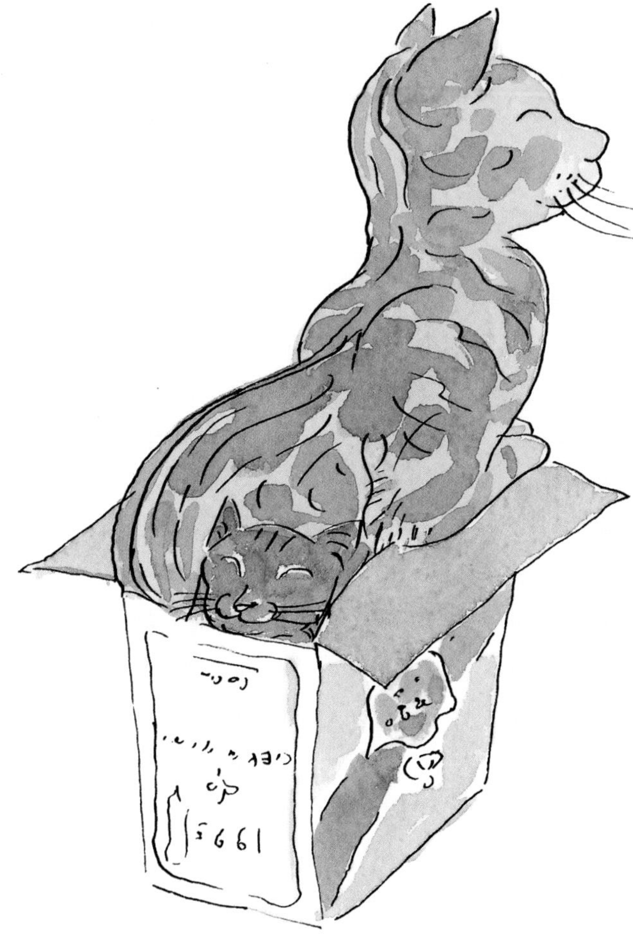

And now Ginger
and the naughty kitten
get along very well ...

most of the time!

MORE WALKER PAPERBACKS

For You to Enjoy

Also by Charlotte Voake

MRS GOOSE'S BABY

Shortlisted for the Best Book for Babies Award

There's something very strange about Mrs Goose's baby – but her mother love is so great that she alone cannot see what it is!

"An ideal picture book for the youngest child." *The Good Book Guide*

0-7445-4791-1 £4.99

TOM'S CAT

There are all sorts of noises around the house – but which, if any, is coming from Tom's cat?

"Among my favourites ... ingenious and very funny."

Quentin Blake, The Independent

0-7445-5272-9 £4.99

MR DAVIES AND THE BABY

Mr Davies is a very determined little dog. He wants to go for a walk with the baby – and nothing is going to stop him!

"Voake's attractive drawings turn Mr Davies into a hero and would persuade the crossest mum to feel sympathy for him." *The Times*

0-7445-5237-0 £4.99